USBORNE FIRST READING
Level Two

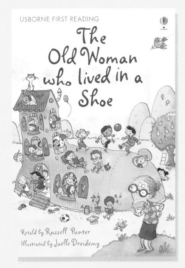

USBORNE FIRST READING

The Old Woman who lived in a Shoe

Retold by Russell Punter
Illustrated by Joelle Dreidemy

USBORNE FIRST READING

Brer Rabbit and the Blackberry Bush

Retold by Louie Stowell
Illustrated by Eva Muszynski

USBORNE FIRST READING

How Elephants lost their Wings

Retold by Lesley Sims
Illustrated by Katie Lovell

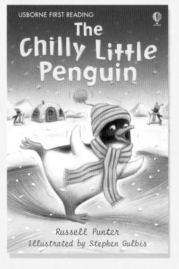

USBORNE FIRST READING

The Chilly Little Penguin

Russell Punter
Illustrated by Stephen Gulbis

There Was A Crooked Man

Retold by
Russell Punter

Illustrated by David Semple

Reading consultant: Alison Kelly
Roehampton University

There was a
crooked man...

...and he walked a
crooked mile.

He found a crooked
sixpence...

...upon a crooked stile.

He bought a crooked cat...

...which caught a
crooked mouse.

And they all lived together...

...in a little
crooked house.

The crooked man
was hungry.

So he cooked a
crooked fish.

His crooked cat
could smell it.

And she snatched it
off the dish.

The crooked man
was angry.

He chased his cat
outside.

15

He couldn't see her
anywhere.

She'd found a place
to hide.

The man smelled something fishy.

So he followed where
it led...

...across his crooked garden...

...into his crooked shed.

And there upon a
sack...

...snuggled up against
each other...

...were thirteen
hungry kittens...

...and their kind but crooked mother.

PUZZLES

Puzzle 1

Can you spot the differences between these two pictures? There are six to find.

Puzzle 2

Find these things in the picture:

cat   fish   dish

hat   chair   window

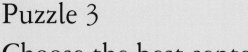

Puzzle 3
Choose the best sentence
in each picure.

I'm angry.

I'm hungry.

Give it back!

Give it away!

Answers to puzzles

Puzzle 1

Puzzle 2

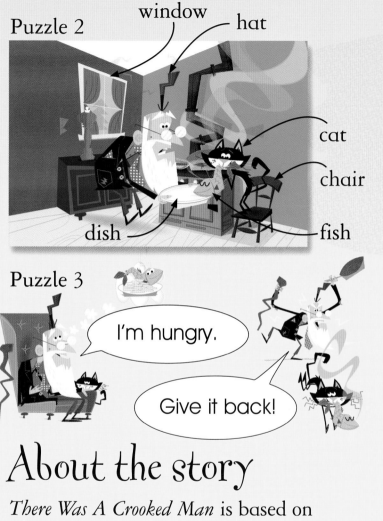

window   hat

cat

chair

fish

dish

Puzzle 3

I'm hungry.

Give it back!

About the story

There Was A Crooked Man is based on
an old nursery rhyme. It was written
about a Scottish General named
Sir Alexander Leslie.

Series editor:
Lesley Sims

First published in 2009 by Usborne Publishing Ltd., Usborne House,
83-85 Saffron Hill, London EC1N 8RT, England. www.usborne.com
Copyright © 2009 Usborne Publishing Ltd.

32

USBORNE FIRST READING
Level Three

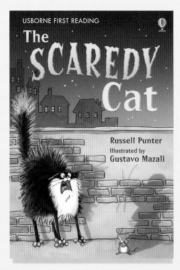

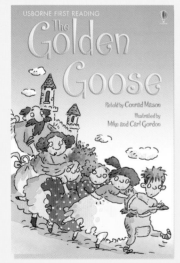